Carnation

With kind regards from the author,
Vickie Jo Milleson

By
Vickie J. Milleson

Illustrated by
Connie Jean Keaton

Carnation

By Vickie Jo Milleson

Illustrated by Connie Jean Keaton

copyright ©2008 Vickie Jo Milleson, Connie Jean Keaton

To order additional copies of this book

or for book publishing information, or to contact the author:

Headline Kids
P.O. Box 52
Terra Alta, WV 26764
www.headlinebooks.com

Tel/Fax: 800-570-5951
Email: mybook@headlinebooks.com

Headline Kids is an imprint of Headline Books

ISBN 0-929915-81-X
ISBN-13: 978-0-929915-81-4

Library of Congress Control Number: 2008931872

PRINTED IN THE UNITED STATES OF AMERICA

In Loving Memory of Our Parents,

Helen Catherine Ansel and
William H. Ansel, Jr., Esquire

and In Loving Memory of
Ralph C. Keaton

With a special dedication and thank you to
William J. Milleson, Sr.

Dedicated to our middle sister
Barbara Ann Ansel Carl and her husband,
Dr. Harold C. Carl, II

And to our parent's grandchildren,
(in chronological order)

Harold Charles Carl, III, Esquire
Helen Catherine Carl Wells
Amy Jean Keaton Haines
Lori Ann Carl Barnhart
William Connard Keaton, Esquire
Julie Ann Milleson Frazer, Esquire
Jill Christine Milleson Puffenbarger
William Joseph Milleson, Jr., Esquire

One day, when I was a young man living in Springfield, West Virginia, I decided to go to The Field to chop some firewood. Beefsteak, my favorite black, brown, and white hound, quickly followed after me.

The Field was a beautiful place. Inside the gate, looking north, The Field was one long meadow. It was bordered on the left by a hillside covered with the lovely sugar maple trees of fall. Red, yellow, and orange trees blazed like fire.

On the right, The Field was bordered by a bank on which rested a set of railroad tracks. Below the tracks, a beautiful little stream of crystal clear water meandered through the fallen leaves. Great oak and hickory nut trees lined the sides of the stream.

Beefsteak, always excited when we came to The Field, took off after a rabbit. I was not worried. He never caught one, and he would return shortly to me.

As I was walking by the stream, I happened to notice a little door in one of the great hickory nut trees. Having walked through these woods many times, I was surprised because I had never before noticed this door.

I walked to the door and knocked. Quickly, the door was opened by an adorable pixie of a girl!

She was small with curly red plaits of hair. She wore a pretty dress of robin egg blue. With her lovely smile, I thought she looked very nice.

"Why, hello," I stammered.

"Why, hello to you," the young girl smiled, "I recognize you. You are the man who often comes into these woods. Sometimes, I see you with three little girls."

"Yes, those are my daughters," I replied, "but, who are you?"

"I, sir, am Carnation. I live here in the woods. Actually, I live in this very tree," she smiled. "Won't you please come into my home?"

So, taking off my hat, I entered her little house.

The door opened into a large room. It was flooded with sunlight streaming through a window trimmed with a dainty yellow curtain. Pretty flowers in a box decorated the outside window sill.

To my surprise, the room was filled with small furniture.

On one side of the room was a bed
with a canopy of blue.

On the other—a little stove, refrigerator, and sink. Pretty blue dishes lined the shelves of a tiny cupboard. In the center of the room there was a little table with two chairs. The walls were decorated with tiny pictures and on the floor lay a bright rag rug.

"Won't you please sit down and have a cup of hot tea with me?" Carnation politely asked.

"Why, that would be very nice," I smiled.

"Well, just sit in that chair. I will only be a minute," Carnation replied, as she busied herself in the little kitchen of her home.

Carnation went to the little sink and filled her tiny kettle with water. She set the kettle on her small stove to boil. Then, Carnation went to the little cupboard which held her pretty dishes.

Quickly, Carnation set the table. It was covered with a pretty yellow tablecloth that matched her curtains. In the center of the table was a vase of the beautifully colored maple leaves.

On this table, she placed two little blue tea cups and saucers, a little cream pitcher and sugar bowl, two tiny spoons, and a small blue teapot. Then, Carnation placed a lovely plate of golden cookies on the table.

Finally, she sat down to pour our tea.

"I hope you like these. They are hickory nut cookies, and I make them from the nuts that fall from my tree each autumn," Carnation said.

I took one of the little golden cookies and tasted it.

"They are delicious!" I replied, "I think they are the best cookies I have ever eaten."

Carnation smiled a thank you and then offered me a cup of tea.

I was curious about this little girl. I thought she must get very lonesome.

So I asked, "Carnation, don't you ever get lonesome living here in the woods all alone?"

"Why, I never think of myself as alone. All the little birds, rabbits, squirrels, raccoons, and foxes that romp and play are my friends."

"The doe bring me their fawns each spring to admire. In the fall, the proud bucks come to show me their great antlers."

"The beautiful red fox often slips quietly through the woods for a visit. Sometimes, though, he does not play nicely with our little friends."

"He loves to play. You should see how high he can jump over a ball!"

"The wild turkey will gobble loudly for his corn if his dish is empty. The little birds like to eat with him."

"Always, the little rabbits are with me. I think they are so dear."

"In the cold winter, the little mice like to come into my tree where it is warm. They will sit for hours while I read to them."

"Every day as the train passes by The Field, the engineer blows his whistle for me, and the conductor always waves a cheery, hello."

"Even your dog, Beefsteak, has been to visit me. We often run and play together."

"No, sir, I am never lonely living in The Field with so many friends," smiled Carnation.

Looking out her window, I knew what she said was true. I could see all the little animals frolicking around her tree. It was very pleasant.

Sadly, I noticed that the sun was beginning to set, so I told Carnation that I must be going home to my three little girls.

"Now that you know where I live, please come back and visit me again. Maybe the next time you could bring your three little girls with you?" she asked.

"Oh, I am sure they would like that very much," I replied.

So thanking Carnation politely for the delicious cookies and tea, and putting on my hat, I slowly walked out the little door.

Beefsteak, having found me, lay sleeping on the ground. As I approached, he slowly rose from his nap to follow me.

All the way home, I could not stop thinking of Carnation. I knew I would certainly be careful chopping wood near her tree. I also knew my own three little girls would like Carnation's story.

And they did.

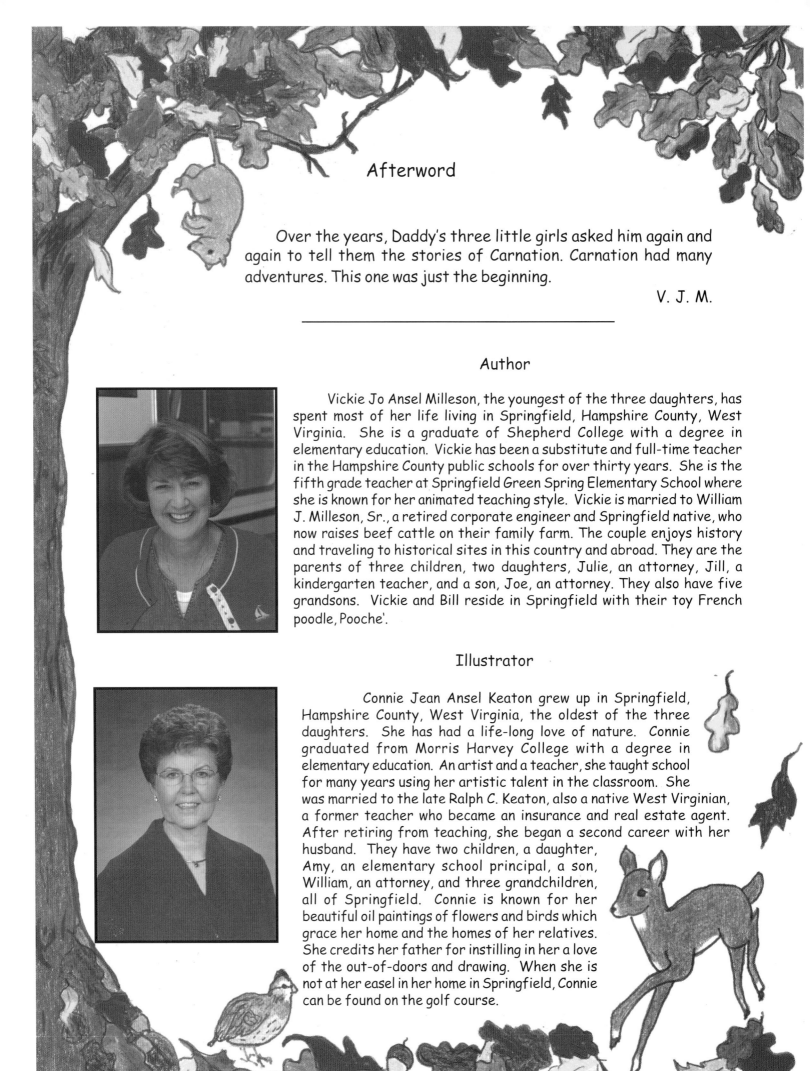

Afterword

Over the years, Daddy's three little girls asked him again and again to tell them the stories of Carnation. Carnation had many adventures. This one was just the beginning.

V. J. M.

Author

Vickie Jo Ansel Milleson, the youngest of the three daughters, has spent most of her life living in Springfield, Hampshire County, West Virginia. She is a graduate of Shepherd College with a degree in elementary education. Vickie has been a substitute and full-time teacher in the Hampshire County public schools for over thirty years. She is the fifth grade teacher at Springfield Green Spring Elementary School where she is known for her animated teaching style. Vickie is married to William J. Milleson, Sr., a retired corporate engineer and Springfield native, who now raises beef cattle on their family farm. The couple enjoys history and traveling to historical sites in this country and abroad. They are the parents of three children, two daughters, Julie, an attorney, Jill, a kindergarten teacher, and a son, Joe, an attorney. They also have five grandsons. Vickie and Bill reside in Springfield with their toy French poodle, Pooche'.

Illustrator

Connie Jean Ansel Keaton grew up in Springfield, Hampshire County, West Virginia, the oldest of the three daughters. She has had a life-long love of nature. Connie graduated from Morris Harvey College with a degree in elementary education. An artist and a teacher, she taught school for many years using her artistic talent in the classroom. She was married to the late Ralph C. Keaton, also a native West Virginian, a former teacher who became an insurance and real estate agent. After retiring from teaching, she began a second career with her husband. They have two children, a daughter, Amy, an elementary school principal, a son, William, an attorney, and three grandchildren, all of Springfield. Connie is known for her beautiful oil paintings of flowers and birds which grace her home and the homes of her relatives. She credits her father for instilling in her a love of the out-of-doors and drawing. When she is not at her easel in her home in Springfield, Connie can be found on the golf course.